Our Community Helpers

Jamie Honders

I0808881

INFOMAX COMMON CORE READERS

Rosen Classroom™

New York

Published in 2013 by The Rosen Publishing Group, Inc.
29 East 21st Street, New York, NY 10010

Book Design: Michael Harmon

Photo Credits: Cover Patricia Marks/Shutterstock.com; pp. 5, 9 © iStockphoto.com/asiseeit; p. 7 michaeljung/Shutterstock.com; p. 11 jan kranendonk/Shutterstock.com; p. 13 Ryan McVay/Lifesize/Getty Images; p. 15 © iStockphoto.com/AlexRaths.

ISBN: 978-1-4488-8917-4
6-pack ISBN: 978-1-4488-8918-1

Manufactured in the United States of America

CPSIA Compliance Information: Batch #WS12RC: For further information contact Rosen Publishing, New York, New York at 1-800-237-9932.

Word Count: 20

Contents

Crossing guards help us.

Teachers help us.

Firefighters help us.

Police officers help us.

POLITIE

Nurses help us.

Bakers help us.

Words to Know

bakers

crossing guards

firefighters

nurses

police officers

teachers

Index